# ZOEY'
## GOES TO THE BEACH

**Written & Illustrated by**
**Todd Churn & Hannah Benbow**

# For Zoey

Here's little Zoey
all ready to go.
Can you guess where she's going?
Does anyone know?

She's off to the beach
for a day full of fun!
There'll be sandcastles, waves,
and a nap under the sun.

With sun block and a towel,
she's prepared for the day.
With her shovel and pail,
Zoey's ready to play.

And after unpacking,
what flies overhead-
but a bright green frisbee!
"That was fast!" Zoey said.

She sees people playing
and having such fun.
What's that in the distance?
It's as tall as the sun!

A gigantic castle
that's fit for a king.
But it needs decorating-
Zoey knows just the thing.

She dresses it in colors
with shells from the shore.
Now the castle is perfect!
But wait, there's still more...!

She swims and dives down
to the deep ocean floor.
There are coral and dolphins
and fishes galore.

She swims to the surface
and back to land.
She heads for the boardwalk
and skips through the sand.

At the boardwalk Zoey smiles
as she pulled out a dime.
She walks to the snack booth-
"It's ice cream time!"

Though she's sandy and wet,
Zoey likes all she's done.
"What a great day at the beach.
I'll come back for more fun!"

Made in the USA
Middletown, DE
20 March 2016